Love Debugged

An Enmies to Lovers Romance

C. C. Washington

First Edition: 2023

Book design: Canva
Book Formatting: Bilalservices(Fiverr)
Cover Formatting: X. Shan

Published by Deems Publishing
deemspublishing@gmail.com

PUBLISHING
EST 2023

Table of Contents

One

Rylan McConnell turned off the engine of his Tesla as he sat in the parking lot of his penthouse suite, his mind still buzzing from the success of the convention he had just attended. It felt unreal; as a young entrepreneur, Rylan had always attended FinTechCon as a visitor. He found himself in awe of the men and women who created revolutionary products or technological breakthroughs every time. He would eagerly listen to their powerful speeches, leaving with a rejuvenated passion and drive.

It was a longtime dream of his to be on that stage, delivering his own impactful message. Today, Rylan gave his third speech at the convention in the last two years and has been honored with an award for his innovative contributions in tech. Leaving the convention, Rylan felt at his peak in success and performance.

"Holy shit," Rylan said with a laugh, mostly in disbelief. Only a few times in his life had he felt this elated and powerful.

Exiting the car, he looked at the time on his phone. It was almost 10 P.M., and his stomach aggressively reminded him he'd barely had anything to eat today. He took the elevator and headed straight for his floor. He recalled the convention as his mind pondered the best thing to grab for dinner. He'd given speeches on security, privacy, and financial policies that directly reflected how he became a successful businessman at such a young age.

His grumbling stomach reminded him that even multimillionaires needed something to eat. He quickly unlocked his phone and scrolled over to his golden goose, a secure payment system that had gained widespread popularity, made waves in the industry, and, most notably, was so easy to use that any tech or smartphone novice could use it.

TruPay had received multiple awards, helping to earn him his lavish lifestyle. He decided to indulge in a simple pleasure, a pizza. With a few taps, he placed his order and tossed his phone back in his pocket. The elevator doors opened to his floor. Walking in, he stared out the windows to the cityscape in the distance.

The ceiling-to-floor glass gave a panoramic view of the city outside that was breathtaking and worth every penny. Rylan walked into the bathroom, taking off his clothes as he walked, ready to shower. He was well aware of the house's emptiness. While many people would never believe that Rylan McConnell was alone most nights, Rylan was yet to find the right woman.

He enjoyed flirting with them, playing hard to get, and driving the overzealous ones in circles. Still, he hadn't found the one person who was for him, and to Rylan, that was okay. He needed to be cautious with his disastrous past with relationships and wealth. As he turned on the faucet, the blast of warm water in his face caused him to rear his head backward as something crossed his mind.

As he'd ordered a pizza from his account, he'd seen a tiny pop-up that shouldn't have been there. It had flashed for only a fraction of a second, and he'd dismissed it, but now having time to process it, he wanted to know what it was and why it was there. Rylan walked out and picked up his phone, finding the pizza was already on its way. His stomach growled angrily. Pushing that aside, he continued his investigation. A glitch had somehow managed to slip into the flawless system he had meticulously built.

Rylan (Frowning) said aloud, "What the hell? This shouldn't be happening."

He quickly grabbed his laptop and logged into the system to investigate further. To his surprise, he couldn't replicate the glitch on the desktop version of TruPay. Concerned about a potential security breach, Rylan knew he had to get to the bottom of this immediately. He dialed the direct line to Caleb White, TruPay's top emergency response expert.

"Caleb, it's McConnell. There's a glitch in TruPay, and I can't seem to find anything in the system that explains it," Rylan explained over the phone, his powerful voice tinged with frustration.

Caleb carefully listened to Rylan's description, his mind already formulating possibilities. "Hmm, that's strange. I'll look into it right away. Give me 5 minutes."

After Caleb hung up the phone with Rylan, he noticed Tanya Lopez, the ambitious and curious 20-year-old college secretary hovering nearby, trying to listen in on his conversation. She was leggy and curvy in all the right places and wasn't shy about using it to get what she wanted. While she thrived on attention and never missed an opportunity to be in the know, she was also quick. She required little guidance, which is why McConnell kept her around at all. Tanya eagerly approached Caleb.

"Hey Caleb, I couldn't help but overhear Rylan's conversation with you. What's happening with TruPay? Is something wrong?".

Caleb looked concerned but cautious.

"Well, there is a glitch in TruPay that *Mr. McConnell* is investigating. We're unsure of the extent yet but are on top of it."

He dismissed Tanya, insisting she let him focus on the problem at hand.

The office was eerily quiet, with only the soft hum of computers and the faint glow of the overhead lights. Caleb sat in the dimly lit room, his eyes fixed on the large desktop screen as he went through TruPay's code. The urgency of the situation weighed heavily on his shoulders. As the minutes ticked on, Caleb knew McConnell's irritation would run rampant if he didn't find the problem.

"Come on, come on," Caleb muttered to himself, his fingers flying across the keyboard as he navigated through the intricate lines of code. His mind raced through all the possible scenarios that could have caused the glitch but couldn't find any irregularities. A few moments later, Caleb called Rylan with his initial findings.

"I've checked the system, Mr. McConnell, but I can't seem to find any indication of a glitch. The app may be working fine." Rylan's frown deepened.

"But that can't be right. I saw the glitch on my phone. It was quick but apparent. There has to be something we're missing."

Caleb, aware of Rylan's expertise, respected his concern.

"I understand your concern, McConnell, but our logs show everything is normal. It may be a momentary display issue.

Unconvinced, Rylan's mind raced with possibilities. "No, Caleb, trust me, something is off. I've been using TruPay for years, and I know when something doesn't feel right. Can you investigate further? I don't want to ignore this."

Caleb reassured him, "Alright, I'll take another look. Give me a few."

As Caleb dug deeper into the system logs, he was determined to find the root cause of the glitch. He scoured the vast amount of data, analyzing every possible angle, but there was still no sign of anything unusual.

Frustrated, Caleb almost gave up, but then he remembered something. TruPay had recently implemented a new feature that recorded more detailed logs of transactions and interactions within the app. Caleb's spark of hope lit up as he accessed the enhanced logs. He finally stumbled upon a clue as he meticulously combed through the data.

"McConnell. It's Caleb. You were right! The new logs captured something. It seems like the glitch triggered an unusual sequence of events. Still, it's not something we've encountered before," Caleb said, his voice tinged with excitement.

Rylan's eyes widened, his curiosity piqued. "What do the new logs show, Caleb?"

Caleb pondered momentarily before responding, "It's hard to decipher, but it looks like some external data tried to interact with the app during your payment. It was quickly rejected, but the app's response to this data triggered the glitch."

Rylan's mind raced with possibilities. External data interacting with TruPay's secure system? That should have been impossible.

"We need to find out where that external data came from and why it tried to interact with TruPay. Could it be a security breach attempt?" Rylan said, his determination resurfacing. I'll head to the office to take a closer look.

Rylan's heart pounded as he jumped into his Tesla, panic coursing through his veins. He couldn't believe the glitch had slipped through his rigorous testing. With steady hands and unshaken dissolve, he sped off towards the office. Every second felt like an eternity as he weaved through the nearly empty streets, his mind racing with all possible scenarios. He knew the potential consequences of the glitch - compromised user data, financial vulnerabilities, and a tarnished reputation. All things he was unwilling to accept.

He couldn't let that happen."Hurry, hurry," he muttered, urging the traffic lights to turn green faster.

The city lights blurred past him as he pushed the car's speed to its limits. His thoughts were a jumbled mess, but one thing was clear - he needed to fix this now. He needed to mitigate any damage this could cause.

Arriving at the office, he dashed to the elevator, desperately mashing the button. "Come on, come on!" he demanded, tapping his foot impatiently.

When the doors finally opened, he stepped inside. He hit the button for the top floor repeatedly, as if pressing it harder would make the elevator move faster. He clenched his jaw, trying to hide the fear that threatened to consume his mind. A clear, concise mind is what would prevail, he reminded himself. As the elevator ascended, Rylan's mind raced through the code, trying to identify where things had gone wrong. He had designed TruPay to be impenetrable. This should not be possible. And that was pissing him off.

Finally reaching the top floor, "Evening, Mr. McConnell," Tanya called out, but Rylan could only manage a quick nod in response. He practically sprinted to his dimly lit office. He immediately sat down, pulling the code on the large dual monitors. Rylan's heart raced as he delved deeper into the code. Lines upon lines scrolled past his eyes as he searched for the source of the glitch. The flashing computer screens around him seemed to mirror his anxiety. Still, he remained focused, his mind working at lightning speed.

"Damn it, this can't be happening," Rylan muttered, becoming more unnerved by the moment. "TruPay is supposed to be foolproof. How did this glitch slip past our testing?" Hours passed, and he found himself lost in the intricacies of the programming language. The faint glow of the city outside his office window dimmed as the night progressed, but Rylan was determined to find the issue.

As Rylan worked tirelessly, he couldn't help but recall the moment he received the award at the convention earlier that day. The admiration and respect from his peers were now inconsequential with the pressure he felt to protect TruPay and its users' trust. TruPay began years ago when Rylan, fresh out of college, embarked on a mission to revolutionize the financial technology landscape.

Armed with a vision to create a platform that prioritized user security and privacy above all else, he gathered a small team of like-minded individuals who shared his passion and drive. In the early days, TruPay was merely an idea—lines of code written on a whiteboard, discussions held late into the night, and endless cups of coffee fueling their determination.

Rylan's vision was to design a fintech platform that would put users' fears about data breaches and cyber-attacks to rest. The team worked day and night, delving into the complexities of cryptography and encryption, determined to build a system that would be virtually impenetrable. They meticulously researched and developed a unique encryption protocol, combining the best practices from cybersecurity and financial technology.

Through perseverance and hard work, TruPay's first version was finally launched. The platform's early adopters were impressed with its security measures, and word of mouth spread like wildfire. As more users joined TruPay, their trust in the platform's security and privacy grew stronger. With each successful transaction, TruPay's reputation soared, attracting the attention of both individual users and businesses. Financial institutions and fintech companies approached Rylan, eager to partner with TruPay to enhance their security measures.

Through ups and downs, TruPay's journey was marked by constant innovation and an unwavering focus on user trust. Driven by his passion and determination, Rylan continued to lead the company with a steady hand, continually seeking ways to improve and evolve.

His thoughts raced, analyzing every possible angle and scenario. He took a deep breath, trying to clear his mind and focus solely on the task at hand. It felt like a battle of wits with an invisible adversary. And damn it, he was still starving. He let his mind wander to the cold pizza at his penthouse briefly before ignoring his growling stomach again.

As Rylan meticulously analyzed the code of TruPay, he finally stumbled upon the elusive glitch. His eyes widened as he realized this wasn't a random bug but a mistake in the code—a slip-up that he had inadvertently overlooked during the app's development. The gravity of the situation hit him hard, and a sense of disappointment washed over him. How could he have missed such a critical flaw? External data interacting with TruPay's secure system? It was supposed to be impossible. Rylan's hands clasped into tight fists as he tried to comprehend the implications of this vulnerability. If it could happen once, what was stopping it from happening again? The potential consequences for TruPay's users and their financial security loomed like a dark cloud over his conscience.

Two

It was 11 o'clock, and Jessie was just about to settle into her cozy couch, ready to binge-watch her favorite TV series with a giant bowl of salty popcorn, when her phone rang. She frowned at the late-hour call, but her curiosity was piqued when she saw it was Mr. McConnell, her boss.

"Hello?" Jessie answered, her voice slightly groggy from the unexpected interruption.

"Jessie Nickols? It's Rylan McConnell. I'm sorry to bother you at this hour. Still, we have a critical situation at the office," Rylan's voice sounded urgent and concerned.

"What's going on?" Jessie asked, now fully awake and concerned herself.

"We have a major bug in the system that's affecting our customers. I've been trying to fix it, but it's more complex than I thought. I need your expertise to resolve it. Can you come in? Now?" Rylan explained, hoping she would agree to help.

Jessie hesitated momentarily, looking longingly at her mouthwatering bowl of fresh popcorn. Going to the office in the middle of the night wasn't her idea of a good time. Still, she knew she couldn't ignore her responsibilities as the lead programmer.

Jessie had become the shining star at TruPay, and her presence was felt throughout the company. Her dedication to her craft was unparalleled, and her passion for coding was contagious. Colleagues admired her not only for being the lead programmer but also for her unwavering commitment to excellence.

Jessie displayed remarkable problem-solving skills in every project she undertook, often finding elegant solutions that others still needed to consider. Her colleagues knew that when they faced a challenging coding issue, Jessie was the one to turn to for guidance. Her work ethic was beyond compare, and she never shied away from going the extra mile. Late nights and weekends were not uncommon for Jessie, especially when a critical problem was to be solved, or a project deadline was approaching. She took immense pride in her work and was determined to deliver nothing less than the best.

Despite the occasional doubter, Jessie persevered and overcame the obstacles that came her way. Her rise to becoming the lead programmer was a testament to her intellect and dedication. She had earned the respect and admiration of her colleagues and superiors alike. She was often praised for her exceptional contributions to the company's success. Jessie's impact extended beyond her technical skills.

She was a natural leader and a source of inspiration for her team. Her willingness to share knowledge and mentor junior programmers fostered a collaborative and supportive atmosphere at TruPay.

Her ideas carried weight in meetings, and her colleagues valued her insights and perspectives. She was never afraid to speak her mind and challenge the status quo, pushing the team to strive for more remarkable achievements. Her commitment to continuous learning was commendable. Jessie constantly sought to expand her knowledge and stay updated with the latest technological advancements. She attended coding conferences, read research papers, and engaged in online communities to stay at the forefront of her field.

"Alright, I'll be there as soon as possible," she finally replied, resolving to put aside her annoyance and assist in resolving the issue.

"Thank you, Jessie. I know it's late. I appreciate your help," Rylan said gratefully.

With that, Jessie got ready quickly, trying to shake off her annoyance at the late-night disturbance. After ending the call, Jessie gathered her things and made her way to the office.

Stepping out into the cool night air, Jessie hopped into her car and started the engine. The roads were mostly empty at this hour, with only a few scattered vehicles passing by. As she drove, the streetlights illuminated the dark, quiet streets, creating a serene atmosphere that strangely calmed her nerves. She used the quiet commute to mentally prepare herself for the task ahead. Thoughts of the day's challenges flooded her mind—tackling complex coding issues, urgent requests from different departments, compatibility problems, and the relentless pressure of tight deadlines.

With each passing mile, Jessie focused on the challenge that awaited her at the office. She replayed her knowledge of the system, thinking about the possible causes of the bug and mentally preparing herself to work alongside Mr. McConnell.

As she approached the office building, the familiar sight of its illuminated facade greeted her. Parking her car, Jessie took a moment to collect herself. She knew Mr. McConnell could be charming and unpredictable, which often made her uneasy, but this was an opportunity to prove her worth as a skilled programmer.

A rush of memories flooded her mind as Jessie sat in her car, gazing at the illuminated office building. She recalled the countless late nights and weekends she had spent honing her coding skills, determined to excel in her field. Becoming the lead programmer had been challenging for her, especially in a male-dominated industry.

Who would have thought I'd come this far? Jessie mused to herself, a mix of pride and nostalgia washing over her.

She remembered the skepticism from some of her colleagues when she first joined the company. Many had doubted her abilities simply because she was a woman. But

Jessie refused to be discouraged. She had pushed herself to prove that gender had nothing to do with her coding prowess.

She'd spent many sleepless nights learning new programming languages, solving complex algorithms, and mastering the intricacies of software development. Jessie had worked tirelessly to reach the expertise she now possessed, always striving for excellence.

I worked hard for this. No one handed me the lead programmer position on a silver platter, she thought, determination burning in her eyes.

It hadn't been easy, but she'd persisted. She had found solace in the lines of code, the logical puzzles that challenged her mind and pushed her to think creatively. Coding had become her passion, and she had embraced it wholeheartedly.

As she took a deep breath, Jessie realized that this late-night coding session with Mr. McConnell was another chance for her to prove herself. She was confident in her abilities and wouldn't let anyone, even the charming and unpredictable McConnell, undermine her skills. *Time to make the most of this opportunity,* she thought.

Walking into the office, she found Tanya, McConnell's secretary, at the lobby desk. Tanya looked slightly surprised to see Jessie arrive at the office at that time of night, but she composed her expression. As she went through the lobby, Jessie felt a surge of excitement. This was her domain, her territory, and she was ready to tackle this problem head-on.

"Rylan is in his office," Vanya said, leading the way. *Figures she's on a first-name basis,* thought Jessie.

Jessie followed her silently, feeling a mix of determination and apprehension. She knew she had the skills to solve the issue, but working late at night with her boss, who had a reputation as a playboy, wasn't her ideal scenario. Jessie made sure her business face was on and checked her focus. C'on *Jessie, there's no room for indecision or self-doubt. You got this,* she pep-talked herself.

As they entered Mr. McConnell's office, Jessie saw Caleb, one of the senior developers, sitting there, looking anxious. Jessie exchanged polite greetings with Caleb. Mr. McConnell was waiting behind his desk with a worried expression.

"Thank you for coming, Ms. Nickols. I know it's late," he said sincerely.

Jessie nodded, acknowledging his appreciation. "Of course, Mr. McConnell. Let's take a look at the code."

As Mr. McConnell explained the situation, Jessie's mind started racing, diving deep into the intricate code web that controlled TruPay's systems. The challenge was indeed complex, and Jessie knew they were dealing with a high-stakes problem.

She attentively followed Mr. McConnell's explanation, her eyes scanning the lines of code on his computer screen as he spoke. As she delved into the labyrinth of programming language, Jessie couldn't shake the feeling that something was amiss.

Just as Mr. McConnell was about to continue, Jessie's eyes widened in realization. "Wait, Mr. McConnell, hold on," she said, her voice filled with a mix of excitement and determination. "I think I see the problem right there!"

Rylan looked slightly surprised but quickly turned his attention to where Jessie was pointing on his computer screen. "You do? Okay, please explain."

Jessie pointed at a specific section on McConnell's computer screen with a focused gaze.

"This line of code here is supposed to call the function that verifies user credentials, but there's a syntax error. It's missing a closing parenthesis, causing the function not to execute correctly."

Rylan's eyes followed her finger as he examined the code closely. He was genuinely impressed by Jessie's keen eye for detail. It was evident that she had a deep understanding of the coding language, and her expertise shone through.

"You're right, Ms. Nickols. I can't believe I missed that," Rylan admitted, a mixture of surprise and gratitude in his voice. "You have an impressive eye for coding intricacies."

Jessie smiled modestly, feeling a sense of accomplishment. "It happens to the best of us. Coding can be tricky, but the devil is in the details."

Rylan nodded, acknowledging her expertise. "You're absolutely right. Thank you for catching that mistake."

As they cited the error, Jessie couldn't help but feel a surge of confidence. This was a challenging task, and finding the glitch was a significant accomplishment. However, she knew that their work was far from over.

"There's more to it than just this," Jessie said, her mind already racing to the next steps. "The missing parenthesis was just one issue. We need to thoroughly review the entire codebase to ensure there are no other hidden vulnerabilities."

Rylan admired Jessie's determination and foresight. "You're right. Let's not leave any stones unturned. We'll work together to review the entire codebase and ensure it's robust and secure."

Rylan quickly asked, "Tell me what you think we should do. How would you proceed?"

Feeling a mix of excitement and hesitation, Jessie replied, "I'd prefer to work on this alone, Mr. McConnell. I can figure it out and see it taken care of."

Rylan's face showed a hint of concern. "I know you're capable, Ms. Nickols, but this bug is critical. We can't afford to waste time. Let's solve it together."

Jessie weighed her options. Rylan was right; this was a high-stakes situation. Reluctantly, she agreed, "Alright, but let's focus and not get sidetracked."

Rylan nodded, "Deal. We need to untangle this bug without affecting the rest of the system or disconnecting our customers."

As Jessie and Rylan continued to work late into the night, her mind wandered to a conversation she had with Sarah, one of her colleagues at work, a few weeks ago. Sarah had warned her about Mr. McConnell's reputation as a flirt and a playboy.

As she stared at the lines of code, Jessie couldn't help but remember her college words about Mr. McConnell, "He's charming and all, but be careful. He's quite the ladies' man. I've seen him flirt with practically everyone in the office."

At the time, Jessie had dismissed it as office gossip. Still, now, working closely with him, she couldn't help but notice his charismatic demeanor. He had an easy way of interacting with people that could easily be misconstrued as flirting.

He must have quite the reputation if Sarah was warning me about him, Jessie thought to herself, a hint of amusement tugging at the corners of her lips.

Despite her initial reservations, Jessie was surprised by his focus and dedication to solving the bug. As they collaborated, she saw a different side of him—a dedicated and knowledgeable professional who genuinely cared about the system he had built.

He may have a playboy reputation, but he's no slouch when it comes to coding, she acknowledged in her thoughts, silently admiring his skill.

Jessie appreciated Mr. McConnell's guidance and insights as the night wore on. He respected her abilities as a programmer and made her feel like an equal partner in their late-night coding adventure.

Maybe he's more than just a charming playboy after all, she pondered, surprised at how her initial judgments were being so quickly challenged.

Three

As Rylan and Jessie continued to work side by side, the tension between them began to ease slightly. Rylan couldn't help but admire Jessie's dedication and professionalism, and he wanted to strike a balance between casual conversation and maintaining the respect that came with their professional relationship.

"So, Ms. Nickols, aside from coding, what do you do for fun?" Rylan asked, trying to keep the conversation light.

Jessie glanced at him briefly, a flicker of surprise in her eyes at the question. "Jessie is fine. Well, I enjoy outdoor activities like hiking and biking. It's a nice way to clear my mind and recharge after long coding sessions."

As she mentioned her love for outdoor activities, her childhood memories flooded Jessie's mind. She couldn't help but reflect on the times she spent with her late adopted sister, Emily, and their parents, engaging in various outdoor adventures.

They used to live in a quaint little town surrounded by picturesque landscapes and lush forests. Jessie and Emily were inseparable, and their parents, both avid nature enthusiasts, instilled in them a deep appreciation for the outdoors. Every weekend, the family would embark on exciting expeditions, exploring hiking trails, biking through scenic paths, and even going on camping trips.

Jessie recalled how her parents would teach them about the wonders of nature—identifying different plants and animals, telling stories around the campfire, and gazing at the stars in awe. Those were the moments when she felt truly alive and connected with her family and the world around her.

"Jessie, then. But then please call me Rylan. That sounds refreshing," Rylan replied, genuinely interested. "I should consider joining you on one of those hikes sometime. It's been a while since I had a chance to step away from the office."

Jessie raised an eyebrow, a hint of amusement in her voice. "Are you saying you're willing to leave work behind for a few hours, Rylan? I find that hard to believe."

She couldn't help but reflect on the persona of Rylan within the company. Rylan was undoubtedly a workaholic known for his relentless dedication to TruPay and relentless pursuit of innovation and success. He was the driving force behind the company's growth and prosperity, constantly pushing the boundaries of what was possible in the financial industry.

Within the walls of TruPay, Rylan was a respected and admired leader. He led countless meetings, driving the team with his ambitious vision and unwavering commitment. His passion for the company was evident in every decision he made, and he was always the first to arrive at the office and the last to leave.

However, outside work, Rylan's personal life was shrouded in a reputation as a flirt and a playboy. He was known for his charm and charisma, effortlessly captivating those around him. His busy work schedule left little time for meaningful personal relationships, and he often indulged in casual flirtations without any intention of commitment.

It was a contrast that intrigued and puzzled many at TruPay. Rylan was a man who poured his heart and soul into the company, achieving remarkable success and earning the loyalty of his employees. Yet, he seemed content to keep his personal life at arm's length, focusing solely on pursuing professional goals.

This reputation didn't deter Jessie from recognizing Rylan's brilliance as a leader and entrepreneur. She admired his work ethic and the innovation he brought to the financial industry. Evidently, his dedication had propelled TruPay to its current heights and made it a formidable player in the market.

Rylan chuckled, appreciating Jessie's candidness. "I know, I know. I may have a reputation for being a workaholic, but even I need a break now and then."

Their brief exchange allowed them to connect on a more personal level. Still, Jessie quickly steered the conversation back to the task at hand. "We can plan a hiking trip later. Right now, let's focus on fixing this glitch."

Rylan nodded, impressed by Jessie's ability to prioritize and remain focused. He realized that she was a skilled programmer and a disciplined professional.

As they worked together, Rylan continued to observe Jessie's expertise and commitment to her work. He was grateful to have her on his team and acknowledged her significant contribution to TruPay's success.

"Jessie, I want you to know that I value your skills and dedication to this company. You're an essential part of our team, and I'm thankful for all the hard work you put in," Rylan said, genuine respect evident in his voice.

Jessie glanced at Rylan, her eyes focused and determined. "Thank you, Mr. McConnell" I take pride in my work and am committed to making sure TruPay thrives." She replied, emphasizing the formal title.

"But right now, let's focus on the task at hand. We need to find and fix the glitch's root cause."

Rylan was taken aback by her polite but firm response. He was used to being more familiar with his employees. Still, he understood that Jessie valued professionalism and wanted to keep their interactions focused on their work.

Respecting her wishes, Rylan nodded. "Of course, Jessie. Let's get back to it."

At that moment, Rylan realized that Jessie was not just another woman to be charmed. She was a formidable professional, and he respected her for it. There was more to her than just her beauty; she possessed a strength and intelligence that demanded admiration.

As Rylan and Jessie continued to work together, Rylan couldn't help but steal glances at Jessie, acknowledging her beauty in the back of his mind. However, he quickly pushed those thoughts aside, recognizing the importance of maintaining a professional demeanor. As they navigated through the source code, Rylan ensured they were in a secluded corner of the office, away from prying eyes. He was cautious not to expose sensitive information that could compromise the security of TruPay's systems.

"Let's keep this part of the code under wraps, Jessie," Rylan said, leaning closer to her, his voice low. "We don't want anyone stumbling upon our solution and attempting to replicate it. The last thing we need is someone exploiting this for their gain."

Several years ago, TruPay faced a significant threat to its security that sent shockwaves through the company. A highly sophisticated attempt was made to breach their systems and gain unauthorized access to sensitive customer data and financial information. The attempted breach was cunningly disguised, and the hackers had used sophisticated methods to conceal their tracks. It was a moment of panic for TruPay's leadership as they realized the potential implications of a successful intrusion. The company's reputation was at stake, and customer trust hung in the balance. In the face of this critical situation, the entire team at TruPay rallied together.

They worked tirelessly, day and night, to identify the vulnerabilities in their systems and fortify their digital defenses. It was an all-hands-on-deck effort, and every department played a crucial role in the company's defense. Their efforts were led by Rylan, who understood the gravity of the situation and was determined to protect TruPay at all costs. He mobilized the company's best cybersecurity experts, engineers, and programmers, including Jessie, to investigate and neutralize the threat. With each passing day, the pressure mounted. Rylan and his team knew that time was of the essence; the longer the breach went undetected, the greater the risk to TruPay's reputation and customers. Despite the odds stacked against them, the team persevered. Guided by their expertise and unwavering determination, they identified and neutralized the backdoors individually, fortifying the company's defenses against future attempts.

Their collective effort and dedication paid off. They foiled the attempted breach, protecting TruPay and its customers from potential harm. It was a defining moment for the company, showcasing its team's strength and commitment to security.

As they emerged victorious, there was a sense of relief and pride throughout TruPay. The incident reinforced the importance of constant vigilance and the need to stay ahead of evolving cyber threats.

From that moment on, TruPay doubled down on its commitment to cybersecurity. They invested in state-of-the-art security measures, regularly updated their systems, and conducted thorough audits to ensure their defenses remained robust.

The attempted breach became a valuable lesson for TruPay, strengthening its resolve to safeguard its customers' trust and financial data. Rylan knew that their company's security was in good hands, thanks to the vigilance and expertise of their team.

As he reflected on that past incident while working with Jessie to resolve the current glitch, Rylan couldn't help but feel immense gratitude for the lessons learned and the invaluable experience he gained. TruPay's resilience and commitment to security were a testament to its dedication to protecting its customers and maintaining its reputation as a trusted financial institution.

Jessie nodded in agreement, appreciating Rylan's cautious approach. "You're right. Security is paramount, and we must handle this with the utmost care. We should discuss the details only with those who need to know."

Throughout the night, Rylan and Jessie collaborated seamlessly, their focus unwavering on the task at hand. As the glitch was uncovered, Jessie's keen eyes focused on its potential dangers. Rylan opened up the integrated development environment (IDE) on his desktop, and both simultaneously started typing commands and running test scenarios to trace the root cause of the glitch.

Jessie leaned in, her fingers flying across the keyboard, using her proficiency in multiple coding languages to analyze the codebase. "The issue seems to be originating from the way the system processes user inputs," she pointed out, her voice calm and composed amidst the urgency of the situation.

Rylan's mind was racing, thinking about the implications of the vulnerability. "We need to enhance the input validation and add more rigorous checks to ensure that no unauthorized data can be injected into the system," he suggested, thinking aloud.

Jessie's eyes lit up with understanding. "Yes, that's a good approach. We should implement a multi-layered validation process to catch any malicious inputs before they can be executed," she added, her mind already formulating the steps needed to achieve this.

They perfectly synchronized, bouncing ideas off each other and refining their solutions. With every line of code, they modified, they carefully considered the potential consequences and meticulously tested their changes to avoid introducing new errors.

Rylan and Jessie's collaboration continued through the night, fueled by coffee, their shared passion for problem-solving, and their determination to secure TruPay's systems. As the hours passed, the once daunting glitch began to unravel before their eyes.

Jessie's proficiency in coding languages and her exceptional problem-solving skills proved invaluable. She identified and addressed the underlying issues while Rylan provided strategic insights and ensured the changes aligned with TruPay's overall architecture.

Lines of code scrolled rapidly on the screen as they made real-time modifications, strengthening the system's defenses and closing the vulnerability. Each keystroke brought them closer to a secure solution protecting TruPay and its customers.

"This is a serious vulnerability," Jessie said, concern evident in her voice. "We need to address it immediately and implement additional security measures to prevent unauthorized access."

Rylan admired Jessie's quick thinking and level-headed approach. "Absolutely, Jessie. We can't take any chances. Let's work on a robust solution to close this backdoor and ensure our customers' data remains safe."

As the hours wore on and the lines of code seemed to blur together, Jessie felt the need to take a short break and get some fresh air. She stood up from her chair and stretched her arms, feeling the stiffness in her muscles from sitting for so long. She walked towards the office balcony with a determined but slightly weary expression, hoping to clear her mind for a moment.

As she stepped outside, the cool night air greeted her, and she took in a deep breath, letting the gentle breeze wash over her. The city lights twinkled in the distance, and for a brief moment, Jessie relaxed and forgot about the intricate coding challenges inside.

Four

As Jessie leaned against the balcony railing, lost in her thoughts, she heard footsteps approaching from behind. Turning around, she saw Tanya, the secretary, walking towards her with a mischievous smile.

"Taking a little break, huh?" Tanya said playfully, leaning against the railing next to Jessie.

Jessie chuckled softly, appreciating the brief distraction. "Yeah, I just needed a breath of fresh air. It's been quite the night."

Tanya nodded, glancing back inside the office where Rylan was working diligently. "Yeah, I can imagine. Rylan can be quite the taskmaster when it comes to work, right?"

Jessie nodded in agreement but didn't feel the need to complain about her boss. "He's just passionate about what he does and expects the best from all of us."

Tanya smirked, a hint of flirtation in her voice. "Well, he seems to be quite taken with you. I saw the way he looks at you when you're working together. It's like he's mesmerized."

Jessie raised an eyebrow, feeling slightly uncomfortable with the topic of conversation. "We're just working together to fix the glitch. It's nothing more than that."

Tanya rolled her eyes playfully and let out a sarcastic chuckle. "Oh, sure, Jessie. Just workin' together, huh? You must be some kind of coding wizard to have the boss man so mesmerized." She emphasized the word "mesmerized" with a teasing grin.

Jessie didn't know how to respond, so she smiled politely and changed the subject. "Well, I better get back to it. The glitch won't fix itself."

Tanya grinned. "You're right about that. Good luck, Jessie."

As Tanya brought them coffee, she couldn't help but notice Mr. McConnell's professional demeanor with Jessie. She tried to flirt with him, as she often did, expecting him to respond with his usual charm. However, to her surprise, Mr. McConnell remained focused on the task at hand, showing no interest in her advances.

Tanya playfully twirled a lock of her hair, leaning closer to Mr. McConnell. "You know, Mr. McConnell, I can't help but be impressed by your dedication to your work. It's so attractive," she purred, giving him a flirty smile.

Rylan glanced up briefly, acknowledging Tanya's comment with a polite nod. "Thank you, Tanya. I believe in giving my full attention to the task at hand," he replied, his focus returning to the computer screen.

Undeterred, Tanya decided to up the ante, subtly brushing her hand against Mr. McConnell's arm. "It must be exhausting being such a hardworking and successful man. You deserve a break, you know," she said, her tone suggestive.

Jessie, quietly observing the exchange, couldn't help but raise an eyebrow at Tanya's persistence. She focused on her coffee, trying not to let the situation distract her from the coding challenge.

Rylan politely withdrew his arm from Tanya's touch, maintaining his professional demeanor. "I appreciate your concern, Tanya, but Jessie and I have some critical work to finish. We'll rest once we've resolved this issue," he replied firmly, emphasizing Jessie's presence once again.

Tanya huffed slightly, not used to being rebuffed in her flirtatious attempts. She decided to try a different tactic, attempting to engage Jessie in the conversation. "Oh, Jessie, don't you think Mr. McConnell works too hard sometimes? I've been trying to convince him to take a break, but he's so dedicated to his job," she said, attempting to create a camaraderie between herself and Jessie.

Jessie glanced up from her coffee, meeting Tanya's gaze with a polite smile. "Mr. McConnell's dedication to TruPay is admirable. We're all committed to the company's success, and hard work is essential to achieving that," she replied diplomatically, not taking the bait.

Rylan nodded in agreement with Jessie's response. "Jessie is absolutely right. We're a team here at TruPay, and we all contribute to its success in our own ways," he said, subtly emphasizing the professional boundary.

Tanya realized that her attempts to flirt with Mr. McConnell were not having the desired effect, and she decided to gracefully back off. "Well, I guess I'll leave you two to your work then," she said, trying to mask her disappointment with a smile.

"Thank you, Tanya," Jessie replied courteously, appreciating the acknowledgment of their focus on work.

As Tanya left the room, Jessie couldn't help but admire Mr. McConnell's professionalism and how he handled the situation. Despite his reputation as a flirt, he had demonstrated respect for her skills and the importance of staying focused on their task.

Just as the atmosphere began to settle, Caleb walked into the room. He had already been assigned a task related to resolving part of the glitch problem before he came to where Mr. McConnell and Jessie were working. He was always eager to help and be involved in any projects at TruPay, but tonight, he seemed somewhat disappointed when Mr. McConnell told him they could handle it together.

"I'm sorry, Caleb," Rylan said calmly. "This is a complex issue, and Jessie and I understand it well. You've already done a great job with your assigned task, and we'll take it from here. You can go home and rest. We'll keep you updated on our progress."

Caleb looked torn between wanting to contribute further and trusting Mr. McConnell's and Jessie's expertise. He had spent hours working on his part of the problem, eager to play a significant role in resolving the glitch. However, he knew that McConnell and Jessie were the system experts and that their collaboration was essential in addressing the issue comprehensively.

"I understand," Caleb finally said, trying to hide his disappointment. "If there's anything else I can do to help, please let me know."

Rylan smiled warmly, appreciating Caleb's dedication and passion for his work. "Thank you, Caleb. We value your dedication to the company, and your contribution to solving this issue hasn't gone unnoticed. Jessie and I will take it from here, but we'll keep you informed of our progress."

Caleb nodded, feeling proud at the acknowledgment from both McConnell and Jessie. "Alright, I'll head home then. But remember, I'm just a call away if you need anything," he said, eager to remain available if they required additional assistance.

With a grateful smile, Rylan thanked Caleb again before leaving the room. As the door closed behind him, Jessie turned to Rylan with admiration in her eyes.

"He's a dedicated team member," Jessie remarked, impressed by Caleb's commitment.

Rylan nodded in agreement. "Indeed, he is. We're fortunate to have such a passionate and proactive team at TruPay," he said, his respect for their colleagues evident.

With a renewed sense of purpose, they returned to the task at hand, their focus unwavering as they continued to navigate through the complexities of the code.

As they continued working side by side at the computer, Jessie found ignoring Rylan's good looks challenging. She couldn't help but admit that he was an attractive man. However, more than just his appearance caught her attention; it was his presence, his confidence.

As Rylan leaned in to show Jessie something on the computer screen, his hand inadvertently brushed against hers. His gentle and deliberate touch sent a jolt of electricity through Jessie's body. She felt her heart skip a beat as his warm fingers intertwined with hers briefly.

A world of unspoken emotions seemed to pass between them in that fleeting touch. It was as if time had slowed down, and they were caught in a moment of intimate connection. Jessie felt a magnetic pull towards Rylan, and for a moment, it felt like they were the only two people in the room.

Their eyes met, and in that instant, all the noise around them seemed to fade away. Rylan's gaze was intense, and Jessie felt a surge of vulnerability. It was as if he could see right through her to the thoughts and feelings she was trying to hide. With a blink, the moment ended. Both of them let it go to return to the work at hand.

As they continued to work, Jessie couldn't help but wonder if Rylan's touch had been intentional or merely accidental. She tried to push away the flutter of butterflies in her stomach and focus on the task, but her mind kept drifting back to that brief moment of connection.

The unspoken tension between them was palpable, and Jessie was apprehensive of every move Rylan made. She wondered if he felt the same magnetic pull or if she was simply reading too much into it.

Suddenly, their bodies were interlaced with each other, their lips engaged in a deep, sensual embrace.

Their tongues fought furiously, trying to get the other to cave in. The game of give and take kept increasing along with tightening their grip around each other, nipping and pulling at each other's lip.

Rylan pulled back for a moment, a smile taking over his face. As Rylan pulled back, he couldn't help but be captivated by Jessie's beauty. Her eyes shimmered like stars, and her warm smile illuminated the room, mesmerizing him.

"Jessie," he murmured, his voice soft, "you're absolutely stunning." The words slipped out before he could think twice, and he felt a rush of vulnerability at his open admission.

Jessie was about to speak when he kissed her again, but more aggressive than the previous one. A moan crept from her lips as his hands pulled and massaged her nipples through her shirt.

She arched in pleasure, awaiting the warmness of his mouth to relieve his hands. Within an instant, Jessie was on her back on the leather office sofa with Rylan on top, pulling off her shirt. Her hands forcefully grabbed his hair. His hands and mouth traveled lower. A Shiver went through her spine, making her shift uneasily as he licked her inner thighs. He swallowed her moan with a passionate, dominating kiss.

While deepening the kiss, Rylan removed the rest of her clothing. Barely missing a beat or breaking their contact, she removes Rylan's shirt and makes quick work of opening his belt. She leans forward and kisses his neck as he shifts her hips to get better access to her warm center. He then slid his body between her legs and hoovers over her, massaging her thighs and running his fingers over her slick core.

Their kissing became more feverish. She sucks on his tongue as he slips it into her mouth. She wants everything he can give. Her hands push his pants down, freeing him. Her hands roam and play. With each soft movement, he groans into her mouth and thrusts his hips toward her. He was done waiting. He removes her hands, holds them in place above her head, and thrusts into her, filling her completely, almost painfully. He gives her a couple breaths to acclimate before he slowly slides out just to push eagerly back in. Jessie lets out a deep moan, begging for more. As Jessie widens her hips to allow him to push further in... she jerks awake.

As Jessie slowly opened her eyes, she found herself momentarily disoriented, trying to make sense of her surroundings. The computer screen's soft glow and the office equipment's hum reminded her of the long night they had spent trying to resolve the glitch. *When had she fallen asleep?*

"Hey, sleepyhead," Rylan's voice broke the silence, his tone gentle and apologetic. "I'm sorry if I got a bit carried away earlier. I didn't mean to make you uncomfortable."

"Can I drive you home?" he asked Jessie.

Jessie's cheeks flushed with a mix of embarrassment and guilt. She remembered the fleeting moment of closeness before she had dozed off, and she realized that Rylan must have taken their connection a little further than he intended.

It's okay, Rylan," she replied, trying to brush off her feelings of vulnerability. "We were both tired and caught up in the moment. Let's just focus on fixing the glitch now."

Jessie couldn't shake the nagging feeling that Rylan might have seen or heard something during her slumber. She was well aware of her tendency to talk in her sleep, and the idea of him witnessing her dream made her cheeks flush with embarrassment.

As they continued to work side by side, her apprehension grew with every move Rylan made. The air between them was charged with unspoken tension, and Jessie couldn't help but be hyper-aware of his presence. Her mind was torn between focusing on the glitch and suppressing her desires. *Good God, that dream was amazing,* she thought. And had left her wanting.

She wondered if he had noticed the subtle changes in her behavior since their moment of intimacy and if he had any inkling of the thoughts that consumed her. But every time she stole a glance at him, he seemed entirely focused on the task at hand, his professionalism unwavering.

Despite her internal struggle, Jessie couldn't deny the magnetic pull she felt towards him. The memory of their shared moment lingered in her mind, and a part of her longed for more, even if it went against her better judgment.

She tried to push those thoughts aside and focus on coding and debugging, but her heart skipped a beat every time their hands brushed against each other or their eyes met. It was like an invisible force drew them closer, blurring the lines between professionalism and desire.

As the night wore on, the tension in the room became palpable, both from the looming pressure of fixing the glitch and the unspoken attraction between them. Despite her efforts to remain composed, her body seemed to betray her, and she yearned for more of his touch.

Five

As the night wore on, Rylan couldn't shake the confusion from witnessing Jessie's sleep talk. Her words had been tender and filled with affection, and he couldn't help but wonder if she had been dreaming about him. However, he decided not to mention anything about it, not wanting to make her uncomfortable or create an awkward situation. However, the few moans she expressed while sleeping had put him in a place of wanting. Once she was awake, Rylan made sure his lower half was situated under the desk and not visible. He didn't need to make her uncomfortable. Or have a sexual harassment lawsuit to deal with.

They continued working deep into the night, their focus unwavering on the task. Rylan noticed that Jessie seemed more at ease with the source code and the systems as the hours passed. Her confidence and skill with the programming language were evident, and he couldn't help but feel a sense of pride in her abilities.

"You're really impressive, Jessie," Rylan complimented her genuinely. "Your expertise with the source code is remarkable."

Jessie looked up from the computer screen, a grateful smile spreading across her face. "Thank you. I've always been passionate about coding, and it's a privilege to work on this project with you."

Her words warmed Rylan's heart, and he admired her dedication to their work. He found himself appreciating her skills, determination, and professionalism.

As they continued to work together, ideas flowed freely between them. They brainstormed and debated different approaches to resolving the glitch.

Jessie suggested, "Let's try implementing a recursive function here. It might streamline the process and minimize potential errors."

Rylan nodded in agreement. "Good thinking, Jessie. Let's give it a shot."

Throughout the night, they worked seamlessly, quickly exchanging insights and solutions. The room was filled with the soft tapping of keys and the hum of the computers processing data.

As the hours passed, Jessie became more at ease with the systems and source code. Her confidence and expertise were evident, impressing Rylan even more.

As they delved deeper into the code, they encountered challenges that required creative problem-solving. They discussed potential vulnerabilities and proposed innovative solutions.

Rylan suggested, "Let's implement a double-check mechanism to ensure data integrity. It could prevent any future glitches."

As they worked side by side, Rylan couldn't help but notice their growing connection. The late hours had forged a bond, and he found himself enjoying their collaboration and the ease with which they worked together.

Despite the fatigue, neither of them showed any signs of slowing down. The glitch was challenging, but their determination to resolve it kept them going.

Throughout the night, Rylan remained mindful of Jessie's comfort, taking short breaks and encouraging her to do the same. He admired her dedication and work ethic but also knew the importance of caring for themselves.

As they continued navigating through the source code, Rylan felt a mix of emotions - admiration for Jessie's talent, a sense of shared purpose in solving the glitch, and a growing sense of affection for Jessie.

As Rylan approached Jessie's table to show her something on her screen, their faces ended up inches apart. The air around them crackled with an undeniable sexual tension, and time seemed to stand still for a moment.

Their proximity was intoxicating, and Rylan found it difficult to tear his gaze away from Jessie's soft lips. He could feel his heart racing, unsure whether to lean in or pull away. He didn't want to cross any boundaries or make her uncomfortable, but he couldn't deny the magnetic pull he felt toward her.

As their eyes locked, Rylan could sense the hesitation in Jessie's expression, and he knew she was grappling with her own emotions. He wondered if she had felt the same desire that had surged through him in that fleeting moment.

For a brief second, Rylan considered taking a chance and leaning in for a kiss, but he quickly pushed the thought away. He didn't want to act impulsively and risk ruining their professional relationship.

Instead, he pulled back slightly, putting a safe distance between them. "I, uh, just wanted to show you this," he stammered, trying to regain his composure.

Jessie nodded, her cheeks flushed with a hint of embarrassment. "Thank you for pointing that out," she said, breathless.

They both knew that something had passed between them, but neither spoke about it directly. Instead, they returned their focus to the task at hand, the air between them still charged with unspoken emotions.

As they continued to work side by side, Rylan couldn't help but steal glances. He admired her intelligence, determination, and how she handled herself gracefully and professionally.

He knew that their connection was more than just physical attraction; a deeper understanding and camaraderie had grown between them. It was a connection that went beyond words, and Rylan found himself drawn to Jessie in ways he couldn't fully explain.

Her beauty was undeniable, and he was captivated by every aspect of her. From how her eyes sparkled with intelligence and determination to how her lips curved into a smile when she was focused on her work, he was enthralled by her presence.

He had never experienced such a strong connection with anyone, which excited and frightened him. He wanted to know more about Jessie, to understand the woman behind the brilliant programmer. He wanted to explore the depths of her mind and soul, to discover what made her tick and what brought her joy. He found himself wanting to be near her, learn from her, and explore their undeniable chemistry. But he knew that he had to be patient, to let things unfold naturally, and to see where their journey would lead.

As the night wore on, Rylan and Jessie continued to work silently; their tension remained palpable. They navigated through the source code, each lost in their thoughts and emotions.

As the hours passed, Tanya finally arrived with coffee and some muffins, a welcome break from the intensity of their work. Jessie and Rylan gratefully took a moment to step away from the computer, their minds still buzzing with lines of code and algorithms.

Tanya tried to flirt with Rylan as she handed him the coffee, but he remained polite and focused on the task. However, there was a subtle shift in the atmosphere as Jessie noticed the interaction. She couldn't help but feel a twinge of jealousy, knowing Tanya's reputation for trying to get Rylan's attention.

Despite the awkward moment, they managed to enjoy the muffins and have a brief moment of light-hearted conversation. Jessie took a deep breath and broke the tension by asking about Rylan's private life.

"So, do *you* have any hobbies or interests outside of work?" Jessie inquired, trying to sound casual.

Rylan smiled, grateful for the change of topic. "Actually, I do. I love hiking and exploring the outdoors. It's a great way to unwind and clear my mind.

A genuine smile crossed Jessie's face as she replied, "I enjoy hiking too! It's so refreshing to be out in nature. I also like reading and spending time with my friends and family."

Rylan took a deep breath and revealed a more personal side of himself to Jessie.

"You know, Jessie, I was raised in an orphanage," Rylan began, his voice conveying a hint of vulnerability.

"I lost my parents at a very young age," he began, his eyes glistening with mixed emotions. "I never knew them, and I was left in the care of an orphanage."

He paused for a moment, gathering his thoughts. "Growing up in the orphanage was tough. It was a place of both loneliness and camaraderie. We were like a big family, looking out for each other in a world where we didn't have anyone else."

Jessie listened intently, feeling a surge of compassion for her boss. She could sense the weight of his past and the resilience he had developed from his experiences. She admired his ability to overcome adversity and channel his pain into a passion for helping others.

Jessie's eyes widened with genuine interest and compassion. "Oh, I had no idea, Rylan. That must have been quite challenging for you. But I can see how it has shaped you into the compassionate person you are today."

Rylan nodded, appreciating Jessie's understanding. "Yes, it was tough, but it ignited my passion for helping children in similar situations. That's why I've started my own orphanage home. I visit there sometimes to spend time with the kids and try to provide them with the love and support they need."

Jessie smiled warmly, feeling a connection with Rylan beyond their professional relationship. "That's truly inspiring, Rylan. I can relate to your love for children. I lost my adopted sister in a tragic accident a few years ago, and since then, I've felt a deep desire to be there for other children in need."

With a deep breath, Jessie opened up about her story. "I can understand how important it is to provide support and care to those who need it," she began, her voice tinged with a hint of sadness. "I lost my adopted sister, Emily, to a tragic accident a few years ago."

Her mind drifted back to her childhood memories and how she and Emily had been inseparable since the day she joined their family. They had grown up together, sharing secrets, dreams, and laughter. Emily was not just her sister; she was her best friend.

"We were always so close," Jessie continued, her eyes welling up with tears. "We did everything together, and she was like a guiding light in my life. Losing her was the hardest thing I've ever gone through."

Jessie took a moment to compose herself before continuing. "After her accident, I felt like a part of me was missing. I couldn't bear the thought of not having her by my side. But in time, I realized that she would want me to carry on and find a way to honor her memory."

She looked at Rylan, hoping he would understand the depth of her loss and the strength it had taken her to keep moving forward. "Spending time with the children in stressful situations has been a way for me to feel connected to her spirit. I know she would have wanted me to bring joy and happiness to others, just as she did in my life. I spend a lot of time with clubs for troubled youths."

Rylan's eyes softened, understanding the pain of loss. "I'm so sorry to hear that, Jessie. It must have been tough for you. But

I think it's wonderful that you've found a way to channel that love to make a difference in the lives of those children."

As they shared their experiences, Rylan and Jessie felt a newfound bond of empathy and understanding. They both carried scars from their pasts, but they had channeled their pain into a passion for helping others, particularly children in need.

At that moment, they saw each other in a different light. They weren't just working on a project; they were two individuals who had experienced loss and had found strength and purpose in giving back to their communities.

As they continued chatting, they realized they had more in common than they initially thought. Both were passionate about outdoor activities and shared similar interests in books and movies. They also discovered that they had received similar field training, which deepened their connection.

The more they talked, the more they opened up to each other. It was as if a wall had been broken down, and they felt a sense of comfort and familiarity in each other's presence.

Rylan genuinely enjoyed the conversation with Jessie, appreciating her intelligence and wit. He admired her dedication to her work and the way she approached problem-solving with a unique perspective.

Jessie, in turn, couldn't help but feel drawn to Rylan's easy-going nature and his ability to make her feel comfortable. She found herself opening up about her dreams and aspirations, something she rarely did with others.

Six

As Jessie accidentally spilled some coffee, a small gasp escaped her lips. The attentive and caring boss, Rylan, rushed over to help with the mess. Their proximity brought a flutter of emotions to Jessie's heart, and for a moment, she felt a surge of desire she couldn't ignore.

Their eyes locked, and time stood still as they stood inches apart. The faint aroma of coffee filled the air, mixing with the tension that crackled between them. Jessie's heart raced, and her cheeks flushed with embarrassment and excitement.

It was as if an unspoken understanding had passed between them in that fleeting moment. Rylan's gaze softened. He hesitated, unsure if he should lean in for a kiss. Their attraction was undeniable, and Jessie could feel her resolve waver.

Jessie crashed into Rylan's arms, her lips eagerly seeking his. Rylan's mouth came down over hers, and her knees gave out under the waves of desire sweeping throughout her body.

Rylan's strong arms held her up, and she pressed against him, wanting him in the best way. He lifted her off the ground, and she wrapped her legs around his waist. Jessie could feel the hard bulge between her legs, evidence she was affecting him the same way. It made her head spin.

He kisses like a god, Jessie thought, causing colors of brilliant light to explore all around her.

The kisses grew more passionate, and Jessie whimpered out of sheer ecstasy. She nibbled down his neck and clutched at his rock-solid chest. Rylan caressed her with his lips, hands squeezing her thighs tightly. He placed her down on the office sofa. Dejavu set in briefly as Jessie spread herself open before him. He removed his shirt, and Jessie gasped, needing him to kiss her again. His mouth reclaimed her's and his fingers skillfully began roaming around her body. He nimbly unbuttoned her shirt, kissing the skin on her stomach as he slowly traveled south to her waiting wet core.

Rylan whispered against her lower stomach, "I want to be inside you."

She moaned, lost in the moment, grappling his back "Please, Rylan."

She pulled Rylan to meet her waiting lips. His lips found hers, and she screamed into his mouth as he entered her. Their hips moved together in perfect unison as he buried himself deep inside her. His hands were everywhere, stroking her and touching her as she moaned. They made love furiously, fighting against each other and uniting in an explosive release that left both gasping and shaking.

As Jessie came down from that shattering climax, she could feel her heart pounding in her chest, the rush of adrenaline overwhelming her. She looked into Rylan's eyes, her own filled with a mixture of surprise and vulnerability.

"I... I'm sorry, Rylan," she stammered, her voice barely above a whisper. "That was a mistake. We shouldn't have..."

Rylan could sense the turmoil in Jessie's voice as she tried to find the right words to express herself. Before she could say anything more, he gently touched her lips, silencing her. He leaned in and kissed her softly, wanting to reassure her that it was okay.

The warmth of his lips on hers sent a jolt of electricity through Jessie's body. It felt so right, yet she couldn't shake the lingering doubts and regrets in her mind. She pulled back slightly, her eyes searching his for understanding.

Rylan gently caressed her cheek, his gaze unwavering. "Jessie, I understand your concerns, but right now, I want to be with you. This feeling… it's a first for me, and I can't deny what I feel for you."

She could see the sincerity in his eyes, and part of her wanted to surrender to their undeniable chemistry. But the fear was there. Fear of pain and disappointment of losing all she'd worked for. It was just so heavy.

Despite his sincerity, Jessie couldn't shake off the walls she had built around her heart. Her past relationships had left her wary of trusting anyone, especially someone in a position like Rylan.

"I... I can't do this," she whispered, pulling away from Rylan's embrace, her voice barely audible. "I'm sorry, Rylan. It was a mistake."

With her heart still racing from the night's events, Jessie hurriedly dressed. She gathered her belongings and made her way to the corner of the office with her bare back on display for Rylan's heated and confused stare. Her fingers fumbled with the buttons of her shirt as she hastily dressed herself. Jessie tugged her skirt back down from around her hips where it had been as Rylan entered her, and she worked to correct her panties. *Gosh, we didn't even get them off first*, she thought. She glanced around, working to tame her hair and straighten out any apparent wrinkles. This will have to do, Jessie thought.

Rylan also stood up from the couch. He pulled his pants over his hips, zipping them up with a sense of urgency, not wanting to waste any time. His hands moved with practiced efficiency as he adjusted his belt, ensuring it was secure around his waist. The previous night's events were still fresh in his mind, and he couldn't help but feel a mixture of excitement and apprehension. Next, he pulled on his crisp shirt, smoothing out any creases. As he tied up his shoes, he couldn't help but replay the intimate moments he had shared with Jessie in his mind. He started to harden again, thinking about her soft skin and those moans. Running a hand through his hair, he tried to tame the slight disarray caused by the night's events and change his thought.

Rylan's expression softened, thinking of her ridiculous apology. Once set, he took a single step towards her, working to gain any space she'd allow. "No need to apologize, Jessie," he replied gently. "I didn't mean to push you into anything. It's just... I felt something, and I thought maybe you did too."

Jessie's mind was a whirlwind of emotions. She felt drawn to Rylan; that much was undeniable, but she also knew the complexities of a romantic relationship in a professional setting. She took a deep breath, trying to regain her composure, unable to find the words to express her feelings.

"It was a mistake," she said firmly, her voice sounding distant even to her ears. "We shouldn't have let it happen."

Inside, she was seething with anger at herself. How could she let her emotions get the better of her? She had always prided herself on her professionalism and dedication to her work. Getting involved with her boss was unprofessional and potentially disastrous for her career.

As she excused herself to go to the restroom, she walked away feeling confused and frustrated. She didn't understand why she had allowed herself to be so vulnerable with Rylan. It wasn't like her to let her guard down so easily.

In the bathroom, Jessie splashed cold water on her face, hoping to shake off the lingering effects of the encounter. But no matter how much she tried to rationalize her feelings away, they persisted, nagging at the edges of her mind. Looking at herself in the mirror, she wondered how things had become so complicated.

Tanya and Caleb found a moment of privacy away from prying eyes in a secluded corner of the office floor. Caleb's eyes darted around, ensuring no one was nearby before he leaned conspiratorially toward Tanya.

"So, Tanya, have you noticed anything strange between Jessie and McConnell lately?" Caleb asked with a mischievous glint in his eyes.

Tanya's curiosity was piqued, and she couldn't resist the temptation of juicy office gossip. "Well, now that you mention it, there have been a few moments where they seemed quite cozy," she admitted, a sly smile on her lips.

Caleb's eyebrows raised, and he leaned in closer. "Cozy, you say? Like how?"

Tanya paused for dramatic effect before continuing, "I've seen them huddled together, working on some project; they seem to linger a bit too long in each other's company."

Caleb's mind began to race with possibilities, and he saw an opportunity to gather information about the glitch. "Have you overheard them talking about anything related to the glitch?" he probed, trying to act casual.

Tanya shook her head, "No, not really. They mostly talk about work, and sometimes, they get caught up in their own world, you know. But I can keep my ears open if you want me to find out more."

Caleb nodded, appreciating Tanya's willingness to help. "That would be great. If you hear anything, let me know. It's important for us to stay informed about any developments, especially regarding the glitch," he said with feigned concern.

Tanya nodded in agreement, secretly enjoying the role of the office informant. "Consider it done. I'll keep my ears and eyes open, and if I hear anything interesting, you'll be the first to know."

Caleb and Tanya exchanged knowing looks, both driven by their motives. Caleb wanted to gain insight into Jessie and Rylan's involvement in resolving the glitch, while Tanya relished the opportunity to be in the loop with office gossip.

Returning to the office, Jessie found Tanya waiting outside, curiosity dancing in her eyes. Jessie knew she must have overheard what happened and didn't want to deal with her colleague's prying questions. Tanya had always been quick to pick up on any office gossip and loved to be in the know about everyone's business.

As Jessie walked past her, Tanya gave her a sly smile and suggestively raised an eyebrow. She then let out a dramatic cough as if trying to suppress a laugh or choke back a comment. She was clearly trying to be provocative and taunting, wanting to get a reaction out of Jessie. Jessie ignored Tanya's theatrics and continued on her way, not wanting to dignify her behavior with a response. She knew Tanya's intentions were driven by jealousy and a desire to stir up trouble.

Jessie knew she would have to navigate this delicate situation carefully. She didn't want rumors and gossip to spread around the office, especially concerning her boss, Rylan.

With a determined mindset, Jessie focused on her work and maintained a professional distance from Rylan. She didn't want her feelings to cloud her judgment or create awkwardness in their relationship. After taking a deep breath to steady herself, Jessie emerged from the restroom and returned to the office. She could feel Rylan's presence as she walked back, and it took all her willpower not to let her emotions overwhelm her.

Settling into her chair, Jessie adjusted her shirt and skirt, making sure her appearance was professional and put-together. She took a moment to smooth her hair, hoping the simple action would help her regain her composure.

With a glance at Rylan, who was engrossed in his own work, Jessie took a deep breath and started typing on her keyboard. She immersed herself in the coding tasks, focusing on the complex issues that needed to be resolved.

Throughout the day, Rylan occasionally approached her desk to discuss progress on the glitch. Jessie kept their interactions short and business-like, not letting herself get lost in his captivating gaze. She was determined to maintain a professional distance and not let her feelings get in the way of her work. As they delved deeper into the code, their hands moved swiftly on their keyboards, typing lines of complex commands. Jessie's eyes darted back and forth between the code and her notes while Rylan's gaze remained fixed on the screen, a look of determination etched on his face.

At one point, they faced a particularly challenging section of the code. Jessie furrowed her brow in concentration, trying to decipher the complexity of the problem. Rylan leaned in closer, offering his insights, and their faces ended inches apart. The tension in the air was palpable.

Seven

As the day wore on and they worked nearby, the lingering sense of their recent intimacy was palpable. Rylan couldn't help but feel exhilaration and uncertainty, unsure how to address what had transpired between them. He decided to take a chance and open up about his feelings.

"Jessie," he said softly, "about earlier, I can't just pretend it didn't happen. There's something between us; I feel it."

Jessie looked into his eyes; her heart conflicted. She took a deep breath, trying to maintain her composure. "Mr. McConnell, what happened was a mistake," she replied gently, her voice tinged with regret. "I think we should both forget about it and focus on our work."

Rylan's expression faltered, hurt flickering in his eyes. "But I can't forget about it," he admitted, his voice vulnerable. "There's a connection here, Jessie, and I can't just walk away from it."

Jessie's heart ached at his sincerity, but she knew she had to be resolute. "Mr. McConnell, we can't let our personal feelings get in the way of our professional relationship," she said firmly. "I don't want things to become complicated or awkward between us."

Her heart ached from the sincerity in Rylan's eyes and the recognition of her fears. She had seen his playboy reputation, heard rumors about his flirtatious lifestyle, and was afraid of getting hurt. Her past experiences with men had left scars, and she couldn't bear the thought of being just another conquest for Rylan. But she couldn't admit these genuine reasons to Rylan. She couldn't let him see her vulnerability, her insecurities. So, she put up a front of professionalism and firmness, hoping it would shield her from being hurt again.

Jessie's mind drifted back to her last relationship, a painful memory that had left her with deep scars. She had once opened her heart to someone she thought was the love of her life, only to be betrayed and abandoned when she needed him the most.

Jessie and her ex-boyfriend Mark started their relationship on sunny summer days. At first, everything seemed perfect, and Jessie believed she had found the one she had been searching for. Mark was charming, attentive, and could sweep her off her feet.

As the days turned into weeks, Jessie and Mark grew closer, spending time together and making beautiful memories. They went on romantic dates, strolled hand in hand through parks, and shared laughter under the stars.

But as the warmth of summer faded into the coolness of autumn, Jessie began to notice subtle changes in Mark's behavior. He became more distant and seemed preoccupied with his interests. At first, she brushed it off, thinking it was just a relationship's usual ups and downs.

However, as winter arrived, things took a turn for the worse. Mark's flirtatious behavior with other women became more apparent, and Jessie couldn't help but feel a pang of jealousy and insecurity. She would catch him exchanging glances with other women or engaging in lengthy conversations that seemed a little too friendly.

At first, she had dismissed her concerns, telling herself that it was just harmless flirting and that he was just a friendly and outgoing person. But as their relationship grew more serious, so did her worries.

Then one fateful day, she discovered the truth. She caught him in a compromising situation with another woman, and her world crashed. The pain of betrayal was overwhelming, and she felt like her heart had been shattered into a million pieces.

After that, she had sworn to herself that she would never let another man break her heart again. She built walls around her emotions, vowing to protect herself from the pain of rejection and heartache.

And now, with Rylan standing before her, showing genuine interest and vulnerability, she couldn't help but feel a familiar pang of fear. It reminded her too much of her ex-boyfriend's sweet words and charming facade, which had masked his true intentions. She couldn't bear the thought of being hurt again.

"I understand your concerns," Rylan said, his disappointment evident. "But can't we at least explore what this could be? I can't deny how I feel about you."

Jessie shook her head, trying to suppress the rising emotions. "Mr. McConnell, I can't. I need to focus on my work and my career."

As the day wore on, Rylan's frustration grew with each passing moment. He couldn't shake the feeling that Jessie was keeping something from him, and he wanted answers. Finally, unable to focus on the work at hand any longer, he stopped typing and turned to face her.

"Jessie, I need to know," Rylan said firmly, his voice tinged with annoyance. "Why are you so closed off? Why do you keep pushing me away?"

Jessie met his gaze head-on, her jaw set with determination. "Mr. McConnell, I've already told you. I'm not interested in a relationship with anyone right now, including you."

His eyebrows furrowed in confusion. "But why? We have a connection, don't we? I thought there was something between us."

Jessie sighed, feeling a mix of exasperation and vulnerability. "Yes, there's a connection, but that doesn't mean I want to pursue it. You have your way around women, Rylan. You're known for being a playboy, and that's not the type of person I would consider being with."

Rylan's eyes widened in surprise, taken aback by her bluntness. "A playboy? Is that what you think of me? I may have had my fair share of casual flings, but that doesn't mean I can't be serious about someone."

Jessie shook her head, her tone unwavering. "I'm sorry, but I can't risk getting involved with someone who might break my heart. My ex-boyfriend was just like you—charming, flirty, and in the end, he hurt me deeply. I can't go through that again."

"Jessie, I don't understand why you're shutting me out like this," Rylan said, his voice tinged with irritation. "We had a moment, and now you're acting like it never happened. What are you so scared of?"

Jessie bristled at his words, feeling a mix of anger and vulnerability. She had spent so long guarding her heart, and Rylan's persistence was chipping away at her defenses.

"It's not about being scared," she retorted, trying to keep her voice steady. "I just don't want things to get messy between us. We're colleagues. You're my boss, Mr. McConnell. We can't let our personal feelings interfere with our work. If things turn bad, it will affect me the most here."

Rylan took a step closer to her, his eyes narrowing with frustration. "I get that we work together, Jessie, but that doesn't mean we can't explore what we feel for each other. Life is too short to keep denying ourselves happiness."

Jessie shook her head, her resolve firm. "You don't understand, Rylan. I've been in a situation like this before, and it didn't end well. I can't risk getting hurt again."

Rylan's expression softened, and he reached out to touch her arm. "I'm not that person, Jessie. I would never hurt you."

Rylan looked hurt, his pride wounded by her lack of trust. "You're letting your past dictate your future," he said quietly. "I thought you were stronger than that, Jessie."

But Jessie pulled away from his touch, her heart aching with the memories of her past. "I can't trust that, Rylan. I can't trust you."

Her eyes flashed with anger. "Don't you dare judge me, Rylan. You don't know what I've been through."

With that, he turned away from her and returned to his desk, the anger and hurt evident in his every movement. Jessie watched him go, her heart torn between wanting to reach out to him and fearing getting hurt again.

The tension in the air eased slightly as Jessie took a deep breath, trying to focus on the work. Just then, Caleb, unaware of the events that had transpired between Rylan and Jessie, approached them with a concerned expression.

"Hey, is everything alright?" he asked, glancing between his boss and Jessie.

Rylan nodded reassuringly, putting on a facade of calmness. "Yes, everything is under control. We had a few hiccups, but Jessie and I are trying our best to resolve the glitch. Thanks for asking."

Jessie stood up and walked over to the coffee pot, pouring herself a cup to help clear her mind with the warm mug in her hands.

Caleb seemed to buy Rylan's response, but the unease in the air remained palpable. Sensing an opportunity to delve deeper into the glitch's complexities, Rylan changed the topic and asked Caleb a probing question about a specific aspect of the code.

As Caleb began to explain his thought process, Jessie, who was at the coffee stand pouring herself a cup, couldn't help but overhear their conversation. Her ears perked up as she caught a crucial detail in Caleb's explanation that triggered a spark of inspiration in her mind.

With her coffee cup in hand, she approached Rylan and Caleb, her gaze focused and determined. "Wait, Caleb, can you elaborate on that part you just mentioned?" she interjected, eager to explore the idea forming in her thoughts.

Caleb glanced at her, surprised by her interest, but he gladly elaborated on the details of that specific glitch aspect. As he spoke, Jessie's eyes lit up with understanding, and she connected the dots between his explanation and some of her ideas from earlier.

"I see what you mean now," Jessie said with a hint of excitement.

"Mr. McConnell," she said, trying to sound composed, "I've been thinking about the glitch we're facing, and I might have an idea on how to resolve it."

"Caleb," Rylan said, interjecting politely, "I need you to handle some other urgent tasks at your computer. Our financial reports need a thorough review, and we also have an upcoming meeting with our investors. I want you to prepare the presentation materials and ensure all the data is accurate and up-to-date."

Rylan's attention zeroed in, curious to hear her suggestion. "Go ahead, Jessie. I'm all ears."

"Well," she began, "it seems like the issue is related to how the data is processed and transmitted between the servers. I think if we restructure the data flow and optimize the communication protocols, it might help to eliminate the glitch."

Rylan listened attentively, his expression serious as he considered her proposal. "It's an interesting approach," he said, "but I'm concerned that restructuring the data flow might introduce other vulnerabilities or potential points of failure. Plus, we'll need to thoroughly test the changes to ensure they don't create any unintended consequences."

Jessie's excitement deflated slightly, but she appreciated Rylan's thoroughness. "You're right; we should be cautious," she replied. "Let's run some simulations and conduct extensive testing before implementing any changes."

Rylan nodded, acknowledging her response. "Absolutely. We must be certain that whatever solution we implement won't compromise the system's stability and security. It's better to be safe than sorry."

Jessie carefully analyzed the system's architecture and asked Rylan probing questions about specific components. He responded with insightful answers, and each exchange brought them closer to understanding the root cause of the glitch.

Jessie took a sip of the warm coffee, allowing the caffeine to fuel her focus. She leaned back in her chair, her fingers dancing over the keyboard as she delved deep into the intricacies of the code. Her mind raced as she mentally visualized the data flow, dissecting each element like a skilled artist crafting a masterpiece.

Suddenly, an idea struck her, and she quickly typed a string of code, eagerly awaiting the result. However, her excitement was short-lived as an error message appeared on the screen. Undeterred, she turned to Rylan, her voice filled with enthusiasm as she explained her thought process.

"Rylan, I think I've found a way to optimize the data flow and improve communication between the servers," she said, her eyes shining passionately. "By adjusting the data packet size and modifying the routing algorithms, I believe we can resolve the glitch and enhance overall system performance."

Eight

Jessie took a sip of the warm coffee, allowing the caffeine to fuel her focus. She leaned back in her chair, her fingers dancing over the keyboard as she delved deep into the intricacies of the code. Her mind raced as she mentally visualized the data flow, dissecting each element like a skilled artist crafting a masterpiece.

Suddenly, an idea struck her, and she quickly typed a string of code, eagerly awaiting the result. However, her excitement was short-lived as an error message appeared on the screen. Undeterred, she turned to Rylan, her voice filled with enthusiasm as she explained her thought process.

"Rylan, I think I've found a way to optimize the data flow and improve communication between the servers," she said, her eyes shining passionately. "By adjusting the data packet size and modifying the routing algorithms, I believe we can resolve the glitch and enhance overall system performance."

Rylan's eyes focused on her, his interest piqued by her idea. He listened attentively as she elaborated on her approach, impressed by her ingenuity. However, after carefully considering her proposal, he gently pointed out the limitations.

"Jessie, your idea is truly brilliant," he said, a touch of admiration in his voice. "But unfortunately, certain constraints might prevent us from implementing it. The parameters I set earlier for security reasons are causing the error message you encountered."

Jessie nodded, understanding his explanation. While disappointed that her idea couldn't be implemented as she had hoped, she appreciated Rylan's honesty and expertise. Together, they brainstormed alternative solutions, discussing the pros and cons of each approach.

Jessie's eyes widen in disbelief as she examines the code, her fingers typing furiously on the keyboard to follow the digital trail. Rylan, recognizing the urgency in her movements, stands by her side, his eyes darting between the screen and Jessie's.

"Jessie, what is it?" Rylan asked, his voice filled with concern.

"It's... it's an exploit," Jessie replied, her voice tight with tension. "Someone has been actively trying to take advantage of this glitch."

As she traced the exploit, her mind raced with possibilities. Who could have known about the glitch besides herself and

Rylan? And, more importantly, why would someone want to exploit it?

Rylan's brow furrowed in concentration as he analyzed the code alongside her. "But how could anyone else know about this? We've kept it under wraps, only discussing it in this room."

Jessie nods in agreement, her heart pounding with unease. "I don't know, Rylan, but this code looks specifically designed to exploit the vulnerability we discovered. It's not a coincidence."

As they dig deeper, they begin to piece together the puzzle. They recall a recent meeting where they had discussed the glitch with Caleb. He had been the first person they informed about the glitch, and now they couldn't help but wonder if he had betrayed their trust.

As Jessie and Rylan dig deeper into the puzzle of the glitch and Caleb's possible involvement, they recall several instances that now seem suspicious in hindsight.

Jessie and Rylan discuss their suspicions about Caleb, their interactions becoming more animated and intense. They lean in closer to each other, their eyes locking in a shared determination to uncover the truth.

"I can't believe he would do this," Jessie says, her voice tinged with disbelief and anger. "We trusted him, Rylan. How could he betray us like this?"

Rylan's jaw tightens as he responds, "I don't know, Jessie. It's hard to believe, but the evidence is pointing to him. We must be careful and ensure we have all the facts before we confront him."

Jessie nods, her mind racing with thoughts and possibilities. "You're right. We can't jump to conclusions. We need to gather more evidence and make sure we have a solid case."

As they brainstorm and recall more details about Caleb's behavior, they start connecting the dots and piecing together a timeline of events. They recall specific instances where Caleb had access to sensitive information and could have potentially exploited the glitch for his own gain.

"I remember how he insisted on staying late through the night," Jessie said, her eyes narrowing. "And the way he kept asking about the glitch during our meeting... it just seemed odd at the time".

Rylan agreed, "Yes, and his dismissive attitude when I first mentioned the glitch to him on the phone. It was like he didn't take it seriously at all."

Their interactions become more animated as they become convinced of Caleb's involvement. They talk over each other, finishing each other's sentences and building on each other's ideas.

"And remember how he was always hanging around your desk?" Rylan added. "He must have been trying to gather information."

Jessie's eyes widened in realization, "Yes, you're right. He was probably trying to see what progress we were making and if he could find a way to exploit it."

Their conversations become faster and more intense as they start assembling the pieces. Their passion and determination to uncover the truth fuel their interactions, and they become a unified force against Caleb's betrayal.

"We have to act fast," Jessie insists, her voice unwavering. "We need to confront him and ensure he doesn't get away with this."

Rylan nods, his gaze never leaving Jessie's. "Agreed. Let's wait for the police, and then we'll handle this together."

Just as they were deep in discussion, the office door swung open, and Tanya walked in, her expression anxious and concerned. "Rylan, Jessie, I need to talk to you both," she said, trembling slightly.

Rylan and Jessie turned to face Tanya, sensing the urgency in her demeanor. "What is it, Tanya?" Rylan asked.

Tanya hesitated for a moment before speaking. "I... I don't want to jump to conclusions, but I've noticed something fishy about Caleb's behavior recently," she began. "He seemed overly interested in certain company files and was always trying to linger around when you both were discussing the glitch."

Rylan's jaw tightened with determination. "Thank you for bringing this to our attention, Tanya. Your observation could be crucial in uncovering the truth."

Rylan's heart pounded as he approached Caleb, who furtively tried to stuff the stolen data into his bag. The atmosphere in the office was tense, and Rylan could feel the weight of betrayal in the air.

"Caleb, what are you doing?" Rylan's voice was firm, but his tone showed a hint of hurt. "Why would you do this?"

Caleb's eyes darted nervously around the room, and for a moment, he looked like a deer caught in headlights.

"Come on, Caleb, be honest with me," Rylan urged, his frustration building. "Why would you do something like this? You know it's not just about the money. There's something else going on here."

Caleb's evasive answers only added to the suspicion that something deeper was at play. Unbeknownst to Rylan, Caleb's actions were driven by envy and ambition.

Behind the surface of professional interaction, Caleb had nurtured a simmering resentment towards Rylan. He was envious of Rylan's success and the admiration he received as the company's boss. Seeing an opportunity in the glitch that had recently surfaced, Caleb hatched a plan to exploit it for his own benefit.

His ambition to start his own fintech company had been brewing for a while and the glitch provided the perfect chance to sabotage Rylan's business and steal proprietary information. Caleb believed that tarnishing the reputation of TruPay and taking the stolen data would help him establish his venture and surpass Rylan's success.

In a calculated move, Caleb pretended to be concerned about the glitch when Rylan informed him. He acted as if he was keen to help resolve the issue, concealing his true intentions from his unsuspecting boss.

But as the night wore on, Caleb's pretense crumbled under the weight of his envy and ambition. He saw an opportunity to escape with the stolen data, thinking it would give him the upper hand in his plan to start a rival company.

Fear and desperation fueled his desperate escape from the office and his attempt to evade Rylan and Jessie. Caleb knew that his betrayal would be exposed if he got caught, and his dreams of building a successful company would be shattered.

But Caleb was beyond reasoning. With a defiant glare, he turned and bolted, leaving Rylan and Jessie stunned. Before they could react, Caleb was already making a desperate dash for the door, clutching the stolen data close to his chest.

Rylan and Jessie quickly pursued Caleb through the office in an adrenaline-fueled chase. Papers flew as they raced past desks and computers, the moment's chaos mirroring the chaos that Caleb had caused.

Caleb's tactics were sloppy, his desperation evident in every move he made. He knocked over chairs and stumbled over cords, his attempts to evade his boss falling short. Jessie skillfully cut off Caleb's path, allowing Rylan to close in. With a burst of strength, Rylan tackled Caleb to the ground, pinning him down as he fought to retain his grip on the stolen data. Jessie quickly came to Rylan's aid, helping to secure Caleb until the police arrived.

In a moment of clarity, she spoke up, her voice calm but assertive. "Caleb, there's no excuse for what you did, but we must focus on resolving the situation now. The police are on their way, and they will handle this. But you need to cooperate and accept responsibility for your actions."

Within moments, two police cars screeched to a halt outside the TruPay office building. Uniformed officers swiftly emerged from the vehicles, their blue uniforms and badges adding an air of authority to the scene. Rylan and Jessie stepped back, allowing the police to take control of the situation.

Rylan's heart was still pounding from the chase, but he knew there was no time to rest. He glanced at Jessie, their eyes meeting briefly, silently acknowledging the situation's intensity.

The officers approached Caleb, who was now in custody, his hands cuffed behind his back. They spoke with a no-nonsense demeanor, their voices firm and authoritative as they questioned him. Caleb, his face a mixture of fear and regret, barely said a word as the police read him his rights.

One of the officers took out a notepad and began jotting down details while Rylan watched as the police meticulously handled the scene, impressed by their professionalism and efficiency. It starkly contrasted the chaos and tension that had unfolded just moments before. With Caleb now under their control, Rylan felt relieved that the threat had been neutralized.

As the police prepared to escort Caleb to their car, Rylan approached one of the officers to provide a brief statement. He recounted the events that had transpired and handed over the evidence they had gathered during the pursuit. The officer nodded, noting Rylan's account, and assured him they would conduct a thorough investigation.

With their work done, the police led Caleb away, his footsteps echoing in the hallway as he was escorted to the waiting police car. Rylan and Jessie watched as the car pulled away, heading towards its next destination – the police station.

As the police left to handle Caleb, Tanya emerged from her hiding spot, where she had witnessed the dramatic events unfold. Her eyes widened with astonishment as she watched the officers take Caleb into custody. She had no idea that he was capable of such deception, and a mix of shock and disbelief filled her.

Approaching Rylan and Jessie cautiously, Tanya stammered, "I... I can't believe what just happened. Is he really the one behind the glitch? I never would have thought..."

Rylan nodded solemnly, his face reflecting the gravity of the situation. "Yes, it's hard to believe, but we caught him red-handed. He betrayed our trust and jeopardized the company."

Tanya looked visibly shaken, struggling to process the events that had unfolded before her eyes. She had always been ambitious, hoping to climb the corporate ladder at TruPay, but she had never imagined such a drastic turn of events.

As the adrenaline began to subside, Rylan felt a mix of emotions – relief, anger, and sadness. He couldn't help but think about the choices that had led Caleb down this destructive path. If only he had chosen a different course, things could have turned out differently.

Nine

As the rays of morning light streamed through the office windows the following morning, Jessie and Rylan remained hunched over their computers, their fingers flying across the keyboards. They exchanged glances of determination and focus, their minds completely engrossed in the task at hand.

Jessie gasped in excitement as she spotted a potential solution in the code. "Rylan, I think I've found something!" she exclaimed, her eyes shining with hope.

Rylan leaned in closer, his gaze fixed on the lines of code Jessie was pointing at. "You might be onto something there," he said, impressed by her keen eye for detail.

They meticulously worked through the code, testing and retesting different adjustments. Each time they encountered a roadblock, they discussed and brainstormed possible solutions, always keeping sight of their goal.

As the hours ticked by, their collaboration became seamless, like a well-choreographed dance. They efficiently communicated, finishing each other's sentences as they worked in perfect harmony.

At one point, Jessie discovered a particularly tricky section of the code that had eluded them for hours. She called Rylan over, and they huddled together, their heads almost touching as they immersed themselves in the problem.

"Wait, I think I've got it," Rylan murmured, his voice filled with excitement.

Jessie's heart raced as she watched Rylan's fingers dance across the keyboard, making the necessary changes. She held her breath as the program ran, and when the glitch finally disappeared, they exchanged a triumphant grin.

"We did it!" Jessie exclaimed, unable to contain her delight.

Rylan chuckled, a sense of pride evident in his eyes. "Yes, we did. You were amazing, Jessie. Your insight and problem-solving skills are truly exceptional."

Blushing at the praise, Jessie gave a modest nod. "It was a team effort. I couldn't have done it without your guidance and expertise."

Finally, just before morning, they were satisfied that the code was stable and glitch-free. They leaned back in their chairs, exhausted but exhilarated by their success.

Rylan turned to Jessie, a genuine smile gracing his lips. "Thank you for your dedication and hard work, Jessie. You're a valuable asset to this company, and I'm grateful to have you on my team."

Jessie smiled back, feeling a sense of accomplishment and pride. "Thank you, Rylan. It's been an intense couple of days, but I'm glad we overcame the challenge together."

They took a moment to savor the victory before leaving the office. As they walked towards the exit, Rylan placed a hand on Jessie's shoulder, a gesture of appreciation and support.

"You deserve a break after all this," he said. "Take the rest of the week off, and come back refreshed."

Jessie hesitated for a moment, touched by his consideration. "Are you sure?" she asked.

"Absolutely," Rylan replied with a nod. "You've more than earned it."

With a grateful smile, Jessie agreed, feeling thankful for the understanding and support her boss had shown her.

As they finally stepped out into the morning light, the weight of the night's challenges began to lift. Jessie headed towards her car after bidding farewell to Rylan and assuring him that she would take some well-deserved rest. The weight of the long night's work was finally catching up, and she couldn't wait to get home and collapse into bed.

As she approached her car, the early morning air felt refreshing against her tired skin. She navigated through the empty streets towards the parking lot, looking forward to the solace of her car. But as she attempted to start her trusted vehicle, a sinking feeling settled in her stomach.

The car, usually reliable and faithful, was having an issue. Its engine sputtered and stalled, refusing to come to life despite Jessie's repeated attempts. She sighed in frustration, hoping it was just a minor problem that would resolve itself.

"Come on, not now," she muttered under her breath, giving the steering wheel an exasperated thump.

But luck wasn't on her side. The car remained stubbornly immobile, leaving Jessie no choice but to accept that she wouldn't be driving home anytime soon.

Feeling annoyed and resigned, she decided to head back into the office. After all, she had left some of her personal items there, and she might as well make herself comfortable until she figured out a solution for her car.

As Jessie re-entered the office, she found Tanya at her desk, typing away at her computer. Tanya looked up as Jessie walked in, a hint of surprise in her eyes.

"Hey, what are you doing back?" Tanya asked, curiosity evident in her voice.

"My car decided to give me some trouble," Jessie replied with a weary smile. "Looks like I'll be stuck here for a while longer."

Tanya raised an eyebrow. "That's unfortunate. Need any help?"

Jessie shook her head. "Thanks, but I'll figure something out. I'll probably call a tow truck to take the car to the mechanic."

Tanya nodded sympathetically. "Alright, well, if you need anything, just let me know."

"Thanks, I appreciate it," Jessie replied, grateful for Tanya's assistance.

With a sigh, she made her way to her desk, deciding to make the best of the situation. She powered up her computer and started organizing her notes from the night's work, trying to distract herself from the frustration of her car troubles.

Unbeknownst to her, Rylan had also decided to stay behind in the office to tie loose ends. Seeing her, he wondered if Jessie had encountered some difficulties with her car and wanted to ensure she was okay.

As he approached her desk, he noticed Jessie engrossed in her work, her brows slightly furrowed in concentration. He couldn't help but admire her dedication and passion for her job, despite unexpected challenges.

"Hey, still here?" Rylan said, his voice soft but warm.

Startled, Jessie looked up and smiled when she saw Rylan standing there. "Yeah, my car decided to act up, so I'm stuck for a while."

Rylan frowned, genuinely worried. "Oh no, that's not good. Let me take a look."

Before Jessie could protest, Rylan moved closer to the car, trying to assess the situation. Tanya, who had been watching the exchange, lingered at a distance, curious but unsure of how to help.

Rylan attempted to start the engine a few times but didn't budge. He opened the hood to check the battery, and it became clear that the car's power source had given up on them.

"I think it's the battery," Rylan said, glancing back at Jessie. "I can give you a ride home if you want. It's no trouble."

Jessie hesitated, her pride warring with the practicality of the offer. She didn't want to burden her boss, especially after their recent awkward interaction.

"Thank you, Rylan, but that's alright. I'll figure something out," Jessie replied, trying to hide her disappointment at the car's failure.

Rylan's concern only deepened, and he looked genuinely determined to help. "Don't worry about it. I don't mind giving you a ride. It's the least I can do after all the hard work you put in the last few nights."

His consideration touched Jessie, but she didn't want to create any further complications between them. "I appreciate the offer, really, but I'll be fine. I'll call for a tow truck, and Tanya offered to drive me home.

Rylan nodded again, his gaze lingering on her. "Alright. Well, if you need anything, don't hesitate to ask."

"Thanks, Rylan," Jessie said, touched by his thoughtfulness. "I'll manage."

Jessie insisted. "I really do appreciate the offer, but Tanya is here, and she lives nearby. I'll ask her to drop me off. But the fear and uncertainty held her back. Instead, she settled for a simple "Goodbye, Rylan. See you tomorrow."

Rylan looked slightly surprised by her abrupt departure, but he replied, "Goodbye, Jessie. Get some rest."

Tanya drove Jessie home, and the atmosphere in the car felt surprisingly relaxed. Tanya took a deep breath, gathering her thoughts before finally speaking up. "You know, Jessie, I have to admit something. I was really jealous of you when you first joined the company. Rylan is such a catch, and I couldn't help but wish I was the one working so closely with him."

Jessie was taken aback by Tanya's honesty but appreciated her candidness. "I had no idea, Tanya. I never meant to come between you and Rylan."

Tanya shook her head, a wistful smile on her face. "It's not your fault at all. I just couldn't help feeling that way. But seeing you two work together and how Rylan respects and values your opinions made me realize that maybe you're not just one of his flings. I think he genuinely cares about you."

Jessie listened attentively, mulling over Tanya's words. She had always been skeptical of Rylan's intentions, but hearing Tanya's perspective gave her pause. Maybe she had been too quick to judge him based on his Playboy reputation.

As the afternoon sun bathed her apartment warmly, Jessie sat alone with her thoughts. She reflected on her interactions with Rylan over the past few days. While there were moments of tension and frustration, there were also instances of genuine connection and understanding.

Was it possible that Rylan had changed? Could he be someone she could trust and build a meaningful relationship with? Jessie knew she couldn't deny her attraction towards him, but she had been cautious due to her past experiences with men who had let her down.

Jessie settled into her living room and turned on the television; her eyes widened at the unexpected sight on the screen. A small group of reporters had gathered in front of the TruPay building, and Rylan stood confidently at the podium, addressing the crowd.

She couldn't help but feel a mix of surprise and curiosity. What was Rylan doing giving a speech in front of the building? She quickly turned up the volume to hear what he was saying.

"As some of you may have heard, we experienced a glitch in our system Tuesday night," Rylan began, his voice steady and composed. "But thanks to the hard work and dedication of one of our own, that glitch has been successfully fixed."

Jessie's heart skipped a beat as she realized he was talking about her. Rylan was publicly acknowledging her contribution to resolving the issue. Her face flushed with both pride and embarrassment, not expecting such recognition.

"I want to take a moment to thank Jessie Nickols, one of our talented developers, for her exceptional work and problem-solving efforts," Rylan continued, and the cameras turned to focus on Jessie's face, causing her to feel even more flustered. "She worked tirelessly to ensure the security and stability of our systems, and I am immensely grateful for her expertise."

The reporters began asking questions, but Rylan handled them with poise, emphasizing the importance of teamwork and the dedication of his employees. As Jessie listened, she couldn't help but feel a surge of admiration for her boss. He wasn't taking credit for her work; instead, he was highlighting her contributions and acknowledging the entire team's efforts.

Once the press conference ended, Jessie sat in silence for a moment, trying to process everything. She never expected this level of recognition, especially not in front of the media. Her mind raced with conflicting emotions.

Jessie settled comfortably on her couch with a warm smile, wrapping herself in a soft blanket. She placed a refreshing glass of juice on the coffee table and grabbed the remote to switch back to her favorite TV program.

The familiar theme music played, and she relaxed, feeling a sense of contentment wash over her. The events of the last few days and the unexpected turn of events with Rylan still swirled in her mind, but for now, she wanted to savor this moment of peace.

Ten

Rylan picked up his sleek and modern smartphone with a stylish black case. He dialed Jessie's number and waited for her to answer. When she finally picked up, there was a moment of hesitation before he spoke.

"Hey, Jessie," he said, trying to keep his voice casual and inviting.

"Hi, Rylan," came Jessie's response, her voice polite but guarded.

"I was wondering if you'd like to have lunch together today," Rylan suggested, hoping she would agree this time.

A brief pause was on the other end of the line before Jessie replied, "I appreciate the offer, but I think I'll have lunch on my own today."

Rylan's heart sank at her response, but he wasn't willing to give up just yet. "Are you sure?" he asked, attempting to sound nonchalant. "It would be nice to catch up outside of work, you know?"

Jessie hesitated momentarily, and Rylan held his breath, hoping for a different answer. "I'm sorry, Rylan," she said, voice gentle but persistent. "I just don't think it's a good idea."

Rylan tried to hide his disappointment, but it was clear that Jessie's refusal had affected him. "Okay, no problem," he replied, sounding unaffected.

As he ended the call, he couldn't help but feel a mix of frustration and sadness. He knew he had feelings for Jessie and admired her brilliance and work ethic. But it seemed that no matter how much he tried to connect with her, she was determined to keep a professional distance.

With a heavy sigh, Rylan decided to leave for the office. As he walked through the office corridors, his steps were more hurried than usual, reflecting his turmoil. He couldn't help but wonder why Jessie seemed to dislike him so much.

Arriving at his office, he settled into his chair, but his mind was far from work. He felt an emptiness inside him, a longing for something he couldn't have. He couldn't deny that he was drawn to Jessie in a way he had never felt before, and it frustrated him that she couldn't see past their professional relationship.

Throughout the day, Rylan tried to focus on his work, but his thoughts drifted to Jessie repeatedly. He wondered if there was anything he could do to change her perception of him, to show her that he was more than just her boss.

As the workday drew to a close, Rylan decided to take a break and head to the office kitchen for a cup of coffee. He needed something to distract him from his thoughts, even momentarily.

Standing by the coffee machine, he noticed Tanya approaching him with a curious expression. "Everything okay, Mr. McConnell?" she asked.

Rylan nodded, offering a small smile. "Yes, just a lot on my mind," he replied vaguely.

Tanya's eyes flickered with concern. "If you ever need someone to talk to, I'm here," she offered kindly.

"Thank you, Tanya. I appreciate that," Rylan replied, grateful for her kindness.

Leaving the office that evening, Rylan couldn't shake the lingering feeling of disappointment. He knew he had to respect Jessie's boundaries and give her space, but it didn't make accepting it any easier.

As he drove home, he found himself lost in thought, replaying his interactions with Jessie. He wondered if there was a way to break down the walls she had put up and show her the person he truly was.

Arriving home, Rylan tried to distract himself with other activities, but his mind drifted back to Jessie. He knew that he couldn't force her to feel something for him, but he couldn't help but hope that she might see him in a different light someday.

As the night wore on, Rylan couldn't shake the thoughts of Jessie from his mind. He felt frustration and longing, unsure of how to navigate the complicated emotions swirling inside him. Eventually, he decided to go out for a drink to clear his head, hoping that the change of scenery might help him gain some perspective.

Rylan grabbed his jacket and keys, ready to head out the door, when he suddenly heard a soft knock. He frowned, wondering who could be visiting him at this late hour. As he opened the front door, he was taken aback to find Jessie holding a sandwich and a bottle of wine.

"Jessie?" Rylan said, surprise evident in his voice.

"Hi," she replied, offering a small smile. "I, um, brought you some food. I thought you might be hungry."

Rylan couldn't help but feel a rush of warmth at her gesture. "Thank you," he said, taking the sandwich and wine from her hands. "That's very thoughtful of you."

They stood in the doorway momentarily, a silent understanding passing between them. Rylan could see something different in Jessie's eyes, a vulnerability and openness he hadn't seen before.

Finally, Jessie took a deep breath and began to speak, her words tumbling out in a rush. "Rylan, I need to be honest with you. I've been trying to keep my distance because I didn't want to complicate our working relationship, but I can't ignore how I feel anymore."

Rylan listened intently, his heart pounding in his chest. He had wanted to hear Jessie's feelings for so long, and now that she was finally opening up to him, he didn't want to waste a single moment.

Before she could finish her sentence, Rylan couldn't hold back any longer. He gently touched her cheek and leaned in to kiss her. Their lips met in a soft, tender embrace, and everything else faded away at that moment.

They pulled apart, both breathless and with a newfound sense of clarity. "I feel the same way, Jessie," Rylan said, his voice filled with sincerity. "I've been drawn to you since the moment we met, and I can't deny how much you mean to me."

Jessie's eyes sparkled with emotion as she smiled at him. "I was scared to admit it, but I can't deny my feelings either," she confessed. "I've tried to resist, but being away from you only made me realize how much I want to be with you."

Rylan brushed a strand of hair away from her face, his heart soaring with happiness. "Then let's not waste any more time," he said, his voice filled with determination. "I want to be with you, Jessie. I want to see where this can go."

Rylan led Jessie inside, their hands intertwined; there was a sense of excitement and anticipation in the air. They settled on the couch, side by side, creating a comfortable and intimate space for their conversation.

Rylan poured the wine into two glasses, and they clinked them together in a silent toast before taking a sip. Jessie's nerves began to ease as the warmth of the wine filled her, and she felt a newfound ease in Rylan's presence.

"So, tell me," Rylan said, his eyes fixed on her, "what are your hopes and dreams? What do you see for yourself in the future?"

Jessie took a moment to gather her thoughts, appreciating the genuine interest in his question. "I've always been passionate about technology and innovation," she replied. "I want to continue growing in my career, maybe start my own tech company someday."

Rylan nodded, his eyes lighting up with admiration. "That's amazing," he said. "You have such talent and dedication. I doubt you'll achieve whatever you set your mind to."

Emboldened by his support, Jessie opened up further, sharing her aspirations and the challenges she had faced along the way. Rylan listened attentively, offering encouragement and understanding. They spoke about their shared love for the tech world and how they both thrived on pushing the boundaries of what was possible.

As they continued talking, the conversation delved into deeper territory. They spoke about their fears and vulnerabilities, the insecurities they had both grappled with and the moments of self-doubt that had shaped their journeys. It was a raw and honest exchange, each opening up and allowing the other to see their unguarded parts.

With every word shared, the connection between them deepened. They found solace in each other's understanding, a shared understanding of the struggles and joys of pursuing their passions. It was a feeling of acceptance and comfort, knowing they were not alone in their experiences.

They laughed and teased as the night wore on, finding a playful camaraderie in their shared experiences. The weight that had burdened them before seemed to have lifted, replaced by excitement for the future.

At one point, Rylan reached out to tuck a loose strand of hair behind Jessie's ear, his touch gentle and affectionate. She felt a flutter in her heart, realizing that this was the connection she had been searching for.

Without any pretense or hesitation, Jessie felt herself drawn closer to Rylan, her hand reaching for his, fingers intertwining again. They shared a smile, a silent acknowledgment of the bond that was forming between them.

Jessie stood abruptly, taking Rylan's hand. She began leading him down the hallway she suspected would bring them to his bedroom, knowing Rylan would direct her before she led them astray. Once inside his bedroom, Jessie pushed him onto his bed, and they stared at each other for a second before she climbed on top of him. His arms gripping her waist, Jessie on top of him, her arms around his neck. As the kiss deepened, she made quick work of his belt and trousers.

Rylan shifted to give Jessie easier access to him. The bulge she felt rubbing her sensitive numb had her grinding on his lap without removing his pants.

They were so ready and quickly worked to undress each other. Jessie felt Rylan's body perfect against hers, their eyes locked on each other as he positioned her on top of him, Jessie still astride him. Rylan slid Jessie down his length. Without their eyes leaving each other, they moved as one.

His hands continued to guide her hips, with her using his shoulders for support. Rylan swallowed Jessie's moan with a slight grin. Rylan's hand cupped her chin and whispered, "Do you know how beautiful and sexy you are?"

The pad of his thumb slid over Jessie's lips as she was about to say something, and then slowly, his lips came towards hers. Her breath hitched, catching in her chest, her pulse pounding, and her heart speeding up.

"Jessie," Rylan whispered. "God, what are you doing to me?" His voice whimpered.

He lowered his head towards her and kissed her gently on her lips. His lips were warm and soft, Jessie thought. And when he pulled away, she opened her eyes. The two stared at each other in the dark for a moment.

His tongue parted her lips, flipped them without leaving her body, and began moving against her. He kissed her harder and deeper, his stubble rubbing against her cheeks and chin as their mouth and bodies fell into a sensual rhythm.

Hours later, a satiated Rylan and Jessie lay in bed together. As the early morning sun gently streamed through the curtains, Rylan and Jessie lay entwined in each other's arms, their bodies still tingling from the hours of passion they had shared. A sense of contentment and bliss settled over them as they lay side by side, their breathing synchronized in the peaceful aftermath of their lovemaking.

Rylan turned to Jessie, his eyes filled with tenderness and affection. He ran his fingers gently through her hair, tucking a strand behind her ear. "Jessie," he whispered, "I can't imagine my life without you. You've brought so much joy and excitement into my world, and I want you to be a part of it everyday. I want us to be exclusive."

Jessie's heart skipped a beat at his heartfelt words, and she felt a rush of emotions fill her chest. She had never expected to find herself in this position, but something about Rylan had captivated her from the moment they met. His intelligence, kindness, and the way he pushed her to be her best self had drawn her in, and now she found herself falling for him completely and unreservedly.

Her voice quivered slightly as she responded, "Yes, Rylan. That's exactly what I want as well."

A smile spread across Rylan's face, his eyes lighting up with joy. He pulled her close, pressing a soft kiss to her forehead. "I'm so happy," he whispered. "You have no idea how much you mean to me."

They spent the rest of the morning in each other's embrace, savoring the newfound sweetness of their relationship. The world outside seemed to fade away as they focused solely on each other, their hearts beating in harmony.

Milton Keynes UK
Ingram Content Group UK Ltd.
UKHW020819280823
427620UK00015B/751

9 798223 556107